Thomas the Tank Engine & Friends

A BRITT ALLCROFT COMPANY PRODUCTION

Based on The Railway Series by The Rev W Awdry
© Gullane (Thomas) LLC 2001

Visit the Thomas & Friends web site at www.thomasthetankengine.com

All rights reserved. Published by Scholastic Inc.
555 Broadway, New York, NY 10012

ISBN 0-439-33836-0

12 11 10 9 8 7 6 5 4 3 2 1   1 2 3 4 5 6/0
Printed in the U.S.A.
First Scholastic printing, October 2001

PERCY and HAROLD

by
The REV. W. AWDRY

SCHOLASTIC INC.

New York   Toronto   London   Auckland   Sydney
Mexico City   New Delhi   Hong Kong   Buenos Aires

Percy worked hard at the harbor. Toby helped, but sometimes the loads of stone were too heavy, and Percy had to fetch them for himself. Then he would push the freight cars along the quay where the workmen needed the stones for their construction.

An airport was close by, and Percy heard the planes zooming overhead all day. The noisiest of all was a helicopter, which hovered, buzzing like an angry bee.

"Annoying thing!" said Percy, "why can't it go and buzz somewhere else?"

One day, Percy stopped near the airport. The helicopter was standing quite close.

"Hullo!" said Percy. "Who are you?"

"I'm Harold, who are you?"

"I'm Percy. What whirly great arms you've got."

"They're nice arms," said Harold, offended. "I can hover like a bird. Don't you wish you could hover?"

"Certainly not. I like my rails, thank you."

"I think railways are slow," said Harold in a bored voice. "They're not much use and quite out of date." He whirled his arms and buzzed away.

Percy found Toby at the top station arranging freight cars.

"I say, Toby," he burst out, "that Harold, that stuck-up whirlybird thing, says I'm slow and out of date. Just let him wait. I'll show him!" Percy collected his freight cars and started off, still fuming.

Soon, above the clatter of the freight cars they heard a familiar buzzing.

"Percy," whispered his Driver, "there's Harold. He's not far ahead. Let's race him."

"Yes, let's," said Percy excitedly, and quickly gathering speed, he shot off down the line.

The Guard's wife had given the Guard a flask of tea for "elevenses." He had just poured out a cup when the brake-van lurched, and he spilled it down his uniform. He wiped up the mess with his handkerchief and staggered to the front platform.

Percy was pounding along, the freight cars screaming and swaying, while the brake-van was rolling and pitching like a ship at sea.

"Well, I'll be ding-dong-danged!" said the Guard. Then he saw Harold buzzing alongside and understood. "Go for it, Percy!" he yelled. "You're gaining on him."

Percy had never been allowed to run fast before. He was having the time of his life!

"Hurry! Hurry! Hurry!" he panted to the freight cars.

"We—don't—want—to.—We—don't—want—to," they grumbled. But it was no use. Percy was bucketing along with flying wheels, and Harold was high and alongside.

The Fireman shoveled for dear life, while the Driver was so excited he could hardly keep still.

"Well done, Percy," he shouted. "We're gaining on him! We're pulling ahead! Oh, good boy! Good boy!"

Far ahead, a *distant* signal warned them that the quay was near. Shut off steam, whistle, "*Peep, peep, peep,* brakes, Guard, please." Using Percy's brakes, the Driver carefully checked the train's headlong speed. They rolled under the main line and halted smoothly on the quay.

"Oh, dear!" groaned Percy, "I'm sure we've lost."

The Fireman scrambled to the cab roof.

"We've won! We've won!" he shouted and nearly fell off in his excitement. "Harold's still hovering. He's looking for a place to land!"

"Listen boys!" the Fireman called. "Here's a song for Percy."

Said Harold the helicopter to our Percy, "You are slow!
Your Railway is out of date and not much use, you know."
But Percy, with his freight cars, did the trip in record time.
And we beat that helicopter on Our Old Branch Line.

The Driver and Guard soon caught the tune, and so did the workmen on the quay.

Percy loved it. "Oh, thank you!" he said. He liked the last line best of all.

Now flip the book over to start another Thomas & Friends adventure.

Thomas the Tank Engine & Friends

A BRITT ALLCROFT COMPANY PRODUCTION

Based on The Railway Series by The Rev W Awdry
© Gullane (Thomas) LLC 2001

Visit the Thomas & Friends web site at www.thomasthetankengine.com

ISBN 0-439-33836-0

12 11 10 9 8 7 6 5 4 3 2 1   1 2 3 4 5 6/0
Printed in the U.S.A.
First Scholastic printing, October 2001

PERCY
Runs Away

by
The REV. W. AWDRY

SCHOLASTIC INC.

New York   Toronto   London   Auckland   Sydney
Mexico City   New Delhi   Hong Kong   Buenos Aires

Henry, Gordon, and James were shut in the shed for several days. At last, Sir Topham Hatt opened the shed.

"I hope you are sorry," he said sternly, "and understand you are not so important after all. Thomas, Edward, and Percy have worked the line very nicely. They need a change, and I will let you out if you promise to be good."

"Yes, Sir!" said the three engines. "We will."

"That's right, but please remember that this 'no shunting' nonsense must stop."

He told Edward, Thomas, and Percy that they could go and play on the branch line for a few days.

They ran off happily and found Annie and Clarabel at the junction. The two coaches were pleased to see Thomas again, and he took them for a run at once. Edward and Percy played with freight cars.

"Stop! Stop! Stop!" screamed the freight cars as they were pushed into their proper sidings. But the two engines just laughed and went on shunting till the freight cars were neatly arranged.

Next, Edward took some empty freight cars to the quarry, and Percy was left alone.

Percy didn't mind that a bit. He liked watching trains and being cheeky to the engines.

"Hurry! Hurry! Hurry!" he would call to them. Gordon, Henry, and James got very cross!

After a while, he took some freight cars over the main line and onto another siding. When they were nice and neat, he ran onto the main line again and waited for the Signalman to set the points so that he could cross back to the yard.

Edward had warned Percy, "Be careful on the main line. Whistle to tell the Signalman you are there."

But Percy didn't remember to whistle, and the Signalman was so busy that he forgot about Percy.

Bells rang in the signal-box. The Signalman answered, saying the line was clear and set the signals for the next train.

Percy waited and waited, but the points were still against him. He looked along the main line. Rushing straight toward him was Gordon with the express.

"*Peep! Peep!*" Percy whistled in horror.

"*Poop poop poop poo-poo-poop!*" whistled Gordon. His Driver shut off the steam and applied the brakes.

Percy's Driver turned on full steam. "Back Percy! Back!" he urged, but Percy's wheels wouldn't turn quickly. Gordon was coming so fast that it seemed he couldn't stop. With shut eyes, Percy waited for the crash. His Driver and Fireman jumped out.

"Oo—ooh e—er!" groaned Gordon. "Get out of my way."

Percy opened his eyes. Gordon had stopped with Percy's buffers a few inches from his own.

But Percy had begun to move. "I—won't—stay—here—I'll—run—a—way," he puffed. He was soon clear of the station and running as fast as he could. He went through Edward's station whistling loudly and was so frightened that he ran right up Gordon's hill without stopping.

He was tired then and wanted to stop, but he couldn't—he had no Driver to shut off steam and to apply the brakes.

"I shall have to run till my wheels wear out," he thought sadly. "Oh, dear! Oh, dear!"

"I—want—to—stop, I—want—to—stop," he puffed in a tired sort of way.

He passed another signal-box. "I know just what you want, little Percy," called the Signalman kindly. He set the points, and Percy puffed wearily onto a nice empty siding, ending in a big mound of earth.

Percy was too tired now to care where he went. "I want—to—stop, I—want—to—stop—I—*have*—stopped!" he puffed thankfully, as his bunker buried itself in the mound.

"Never mind, Percy," said the workmen as they dug him out, "You shall have a drink and some coal, and then you'll feel better."

Presently Gordon arrived. "Well done, Percy. You started so quickly that you stopped a nasty accident."

"I'm sorry I was cheeky," said Percy, "you were clever to stop."

Percy now works in the yard and finds coaches for the trains. He is still cheeky because he is that sort of engine, but he is always *most* careful when he goes on the main line.

Now flip the book over to start another Thomas & Friends adventure.